Wynken, Blynken, and Nod

Wynken, Blynken, and Nod

by EUGENE FIELD

illustrated by SUSAN JEFFERS

E. P. DUTTON · NEW YORK

for Nanny and Auntie Lor
with love

"Wynken, Blynken, and Nod," a poem by Eugene Field
Illustrations copyright © 1982 by Susan Jeffers
All rights reserved.
Unicorn is a registered trademark of E. P. Dutton
Library of Congress number 82-2434
ISBN 0-140-54794-0
Published in the United States by E. P. Dutton,
a division of Penguin Books USA Inc.

Editor: Ann Durell   Designer: Riki Levinson
Printed in Hong Kong by South China Printing Co.
10 9 8 7 6   COBE

Wynken, Blynken, and Nod one night
Sailed off in a wooden shoe—

Sailed on a river of crystal light,
Into a sea of dew.

"Where are you going, and what do you wish?"
The old moon asked the three.

"We have come to fish for the herring fish
That live in this beautiful sea.

Nets of silver and gold have we!"
Said Wynken, Blynken, and Nod.

The old moon laughed and sang a song
As they rocked in the wooden shoe,

And the wind that sped them all night long
Ruffled the waves of dew.

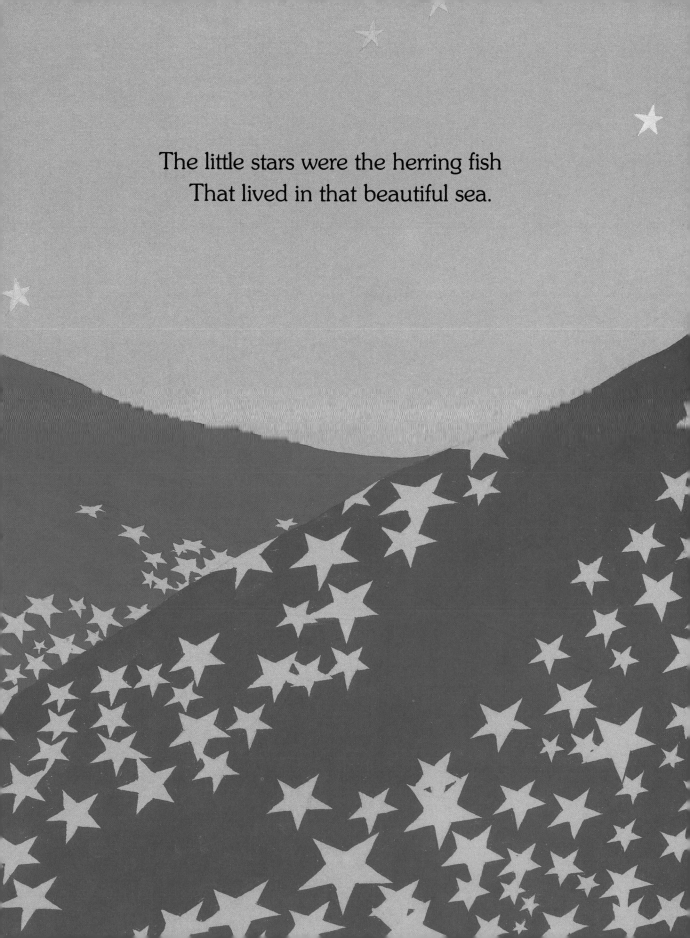

The little stars were the herring fish
That lived in that beautiful sea.

"Now cast your nets wherever you wish—
    Never afeard are we!"
So cried the stars to the fishermen three:
    Wynken, Blynken, and Nod.

All night long their nets they threw
    To the stars in the twinkling foam.

Then down from the skies came the wooden shoe,
Bringing the fishermen home.

'Twas all so pretty a sail, it seemed
    As if it could not be;
And some folks thought 'twas a dream they'd dreamed
    Of sailing that beautiful sea.

But I shall name you the fishermen three:
Wynken, Blynken, and Nod.

Wynken and Blynken are two little eyes,
And Nod is a little head,
And the wooden shoe that sailed the skies
Is a wee one's trundle bed.

So shut your eyes while Daddy sings
Of wonderful sights that be,
And you shall see the beautiful things
As you rock on the misty sea

Where the old shoe rocked the fishermen three:
Wynken, Blynken, and Nod.